**Anonymous**

# A Word of Encouragement to the Friends of Truth

SALZWASSER
VERLAG

**Anonymous**

# A Word of Encouragement to the Friends of Truth

Reprint of the original, first published in 1859.

1st Edition 2022  |  ISBN: 978-3-37512-444-1

Verlag (Publisher): Salzwasser Verlag GmbH, Zeilweg 44, 60439 Frankfurt, Deutschland
Vertretungsberechtigt (Authorized to represent): E. Roepke, Zeilweg 44, 60439 Frankfurt, Deutschland
Druck (Print): Books on Demand GmbH, In de Tarpen 42, 22848 Norderstedt, Deutschland

A

# WORD OF ENCOURAGEMENT

TO THE

# FRIENDS OF TRUTH.

"Let Israel hope in the Lord, for with the Lord there is mercy, and with him is plenteous redemption, and he shall redeem Israel from all his iniquities."

———

PHILADELPHIA.

1859.

# A WORD OF ENCOURAGEMENT.

As the mighty arm of Him who first gathered us out of the world and its spirit, to be " a peculiar people, zealous of good works," is still extended for our help and preservation—for the promotion of the welfare of Zion, and the enlargement of her borders,—there is no cause for discouragement to those whose trust and confidence are in him alone; for he remains to be the invincible Captain of our salvation, who is going on with his blessed work in the hearts of his people, conquering, and to conquer, until the kingdoms of this world become the kingdoms of our Lord and his Christ, to the glory of God in the highest, and the establishment of peace on earth and good-will to men. As he who is the head of his living body continues to be unchangeably the same, and his wisdom, power, and mercy undiminished, infinite, and ever-enduring, there is no good ground for the belief, or the fear, that the testimonies committed to us for our support will ever be permitted to fall to the ground, however many may forsake them, by turning aside to lying vanities; and we have reason to be encouraged and thankful in the well-grounded belief, that *many* are yet preserved amongst us, who are preferring to suffer affliction with the people of God, to enjoying the pleasure of sin for a season, are made willing to continue with Christ in his temptations, for his body's sake, which is his Church, and enabled to detect and withstand the subtle wiles of the evil one, who fain would persuade us that the mission of the disciples of Christ is accomplished, so that we are now at liberty to return to the doctrines, customs, and fashions of the world about us, adopting its *spirit*, manners, and language, even as those of old when the Prophet Elijah was led to take so dark a view of the state of the Church of God, as to believe, and complain, that he alone was left, and that even his life was in jeopardy. But let us remember, for our encouragement, the gracious and comforting assurance that was given to the desponding prophet, at this sorrowful juncture, when libertinism, time-serving, and persecution, so far prevailed, as, in his view, to almost dismember the visible and militant Church; for we may believe it is alike applicable to the apparently discouraging state of things in the present day, when so many seem to have forsaken the standard of Truth, for the exercise of their own wisdom and wills, walking in ways of their own choosing, and seeking the good of themselves, and to promote the welfare of the Church, by means of *their own* devising, not willing to tarry at Jerusalem until endued with power from on high—to abide under secret exercise until the helping Hand is stretched forth for their deliverance from bondage to the sin and corruption of *their own* hearts, until a separation of the precious from the vile is wrought for them, that they may be enabled to go forward, under the holy anointing, and at the Divine command, without offence either to God or his anointed, or the consciousness of there being aught against them which should stand in the way of the exercise of their gift, either in the ministry, or the administration of the discipline of the Church. While a cloud rests upon the Tabernacle, we are required to stand still. If in such a case we go forward, it is at the peril of our spiritual life, and to the endangering of the same in others, within the sphere of our influence.

O, the utter impotency of human wisdom and power to effect, or even promote, the work of reformation—to prepare the heart for the reception and reign of the Prince of Peace, whose kingdom is not of this world, that his servants should seek to devour one another by bitter contention, and unholy strife and persecution; but an inward and peaceable kingdom, set up and established *in the hearts* of those who are subjects to His blessed and holy will, following the direction of his holy Spirit whithersoever this may lead them, having no confidence in the flesh, nor any desire after lordship or outward masteries, but rather after *the dominion of life in their own hearts,* for which they are daily exercised in watching unto prayer.

"The foundation of God standeth sure, having this seal: the Lord knoweth them that are his," though Abraham may be ignorant of them, and Israel acknowledge them not. We may deceive ourselves and others in respect to the state of our own hearts, but the Searcher of hearts we cannot deceive. We may be possessed of a feeling of wholeness, and so profess and dissemble as to deceive, if it were possible, the very elect, and yet be estranged from the love of God, and from the true evidence of our having passed from death unto life, which is found in the *unfeigned* love of the brethren.

The Gospel dispensation being a dispensation of mercy to the souls of men, those who are living under it are bound by the very nature of it to the exercise of kindness, forbearance, and love, even to our enemies, and to those who oppose themselves by the entertainment and indulgence of the spirit of the world, which is at enmity with God, leading into errors upon the *right* hand as well as on the *left;* and any other course is sure to bring down the judgments of heaven upon us for assuming to ourselves the prerogative of Him who hath ordained that we should avenge not ourselves, declaring that vengeance is his, and he will repay—that as we mete to others, so shall it be measured to us again—that with what judgment we judge we shall be judged, and that they shall receive judgment without mercy, who have shown no mercy.

Seeing, then, that these things are so, how vain is all our outward profession of love for the truth, and of standing for its testimonies, while the spirit of vindictiveness, accusation, and faultfinding is found lurking in our bosoms, leading us to defame and persecute those who may have erred from the truth, or by whom we may have been slighted or injured, under the profession of contending for the faith, while we are practically denying it by a resort to carnal weapons, instead of obeying the Divine injunction to " overcome evil with good ?" What will all our adherence to outward simplicity and plainness, and pleading for them, and all our outward show of worship avail us, if our hearts are set upon seeking worldly riches, honor, and pleasures, or punishing our own, or Truth's enemies, even to the trampling under foot of our Christian Discipline, and sacrificing the peace of society to the accomplishment of our own wills ?

Let us seek to try the spirits which are amongst us, that we may be able to distinguish between the wisdom from above, and that which *is* from beneath, lest we be suffered to become as wolves in sheep's clothing, as whited sepulchres full of dead men's bones. Let us prove our own selves, whether we be in the faith of Christ, which overcometh the world, or in that which is overcome by the world and its spirit, as was that of the disciple who smote the servant of the high priest in vindication' of the blessed Master; which act of presumption was followed by the unalterable decree, that "he that taketh the sword shall perish with the sword."

How often has this been verified in the experience of the over-zealous advocate of truth, who, for his unmerciful dealings with the erring, or those who may have not been able to see eye to eye with himself, has been permitted to fall into temptation, until, through persisting in a pharisaical and self-righteous course of censure and persecution, hardening his neck against the reproofs of instruction, judgment has overtaken him, and he has partaken of a full measure of that which he has meted unto others. How often has this been witnessed in the experience of those who have set themselves in the seat of judgment over their brethren, carrying themselves aloft because of an apprehended superiority, and holding themselves aloof from those whose views of propriety were not in harmony with their own, even as Peter did before his memorable vision, by which he was taught to "call no man unclean," and shown that the Holy Ghost was shed upon the Gentiles as well as upon the Jews; both alike being heirs of the same blessed inheritance, under the universal dispensation of Divine grace, wherein the love of the Gospel extends to the very ends of the earth, enabling the Apostles to declare that "where sin abounds there doth grace much more abound;" a doctrine which we gladly recognize as applying to ourselves, when under conviction for sin, and which is equally applicable to others, making it of binding obligation upon the servant of Christ to seek to restore the wanderer and bind up the broken-hearted, which is the effect of the operation of the Holy Spirit, in and through us, as the objects and instruments of Divine mercy.

If any man sin, saith the Apostle, we have an Advocate with the Father, even Jesus Christ the righteous. Wherefore then should we seek to destroy the hope of the erring in the mercy of God in Christ Jesus—which is freely shown to every repenting soul—by bitter denunciation, and an unholy endeavor to bring them under the cruel and disheartening power of accusation and reproach? Is the servant above his master, or the disciple above his lord, that he should spurn and resist the pleadings of the Holy Spirit for those who are out of the right way, or resort to violence and force for their punishment, rather than persuasion and entreaty for their recovery? Having known the terrors of the Lord for sin, therefore, saith the Apostle, we persuade men. He had been a persecutor of the Church of Christ, for which cause he was made blind to the wisdom whereby he had been made to believe he was doing God service by the cruel exercise of lordship and oppression, until, through the restoring power of Truth, he was convinced of his error and induced to pursue an *opposite* course.

The power of the Gospel has ever been a convincing and persuasive one, wherein it has differed from the spirit of the world, which seeks to establish the truth by violence and force—holding it in unrighteousness—slaying the just and inward witness, through the exercise of enmity and ill-will. This is the fruit of the religion of the world, which has ever stood opposed to that of the heart, bringing forth the evil fruits of enmity, contention, and strife, which are attended with confusion, and every evil work, to the diverting of the mind from the work of righteousness through the *gentle, peaceable*, and *uniting* influence and operation of the Holy Spirit, which breathes peace on earth and good-will to men, and the desire for the conversion or restoration of every son and daughter of Adam.

Under the inspiration of this holy power, how many have been made willing to spend and be spent in the blessed cause of gathering souls unto Christ, through the exercise of that charity which shuns any just occasion of offence either to Jew or Gentile, and seeks to be made all things to all men, not to secure human favor or praise, or the exaltation of self, but in order to win unto Christ the hearts of all flesh, according to the Divine will and purpose, even that all should be brought into the unity of the Spirit in the bond of peace, through the knowledge of God and Jesus Christ whom he hath sent, which is declared to be life eternal.

This is the purpose and work of the Holy Spirit, either through instrumental means, or by the *immediate* influences of its redeeming and saving power, which is *now going forward in the hearts of the people*, notwithstanding all the hindrances of our common enemy, who is seeking to divert our minds from that *inward* state of watchfulness unto prayer wherein our strength and safety consist, and turn our attention *outward* to visible helps, or apparent causes of discouragement, in order to frustrate the grace of God, by hindering the promulgation and spread of the Gospel—to retard the coming of Christ's kingdom in our hearts.

The following exhortations, testimonies, and warnings of that faithful and gifted servant of the Most High, Isaac Pennington, may prove an encouragement to the exercised travellers in the present day who are seeking to walk in the way that leads to rest and peace—to know of having their treasure where moth and rust cannot corrupt, nor thieves break through and steal—of sitting under their own vine and fig tree, where none can harm or make afraid—of dwelling in that quiet habitation where the glorious Lord will be unto us a place of broad rivers and streams, wherein shall go no galley with oars, neither shall gallant ship pass thereby, nor the lion's whelp or any ravenous beast tread therein.

"O, my friends, that ye might know and hear the voice of the Preserver! so shall ye be preserved and kept from the voice of the stranger, which draweth aside from the pure principle of life, and the *true* feeling sense. There is *that* near you which watcheth to betray. O, the God of my life, joy, peace, and hope watch over your souls, and deliver you from the advantages which at any time it hath against any of you! The seed which God hath sown in you is pure and precious. O, that it may be found living in you, and ye abiding in it! O, that *no other* seed may, *at any time*, usurp authority over it! but that ye may know the authority and pure truth which is of God, and therein stand in the *pure* dominion over all that is against him. Out of that ye will easily become a prey, and set up darkness for light, and account light darkness; and then a *wrong wisdom, confidence,* and *conceitedness* will get up in you, and lead you *far* out of the way and spirit of truth. O, my dear Friends! that *that* may be *kept down* in you, which is *forward* to judge, to approve or disapprove; and may the *weighty* judgment of the seed be waited for. And, O! do not judge, do not judge, before the light of day shine in you, and give forth the judgment; but stand and walk in *fear* and *humility*, and *tenderness of spirit*, and *silence of flesh*, that the Lord be not provoked against any of you, to *give you up to a wrong sense and judgment*, to the hurt of your souls. And mind *your own states*, and the feelings of life in *your own vessels;* which will keep you pure, precious, and chaste in the eye of the Lord. And, O, do not meddle with *talking about others,* which eats out the inward life, and may exalt your spirits out of your place. Be as the weaned child, simple, naked, meek, humble, tender, *easily led by*, and *subjected to the Father;* so will ye grow *in* that which *is* of God, and be preserved *out of* that which hunteth after the pure life, to betray and destroy it.

"Ye must die to *your own wisdom,* if ye will ever be born of, and walk in the wisdom of God. Yea, ye must die to *that* part that is *so active* from and in *that* wisdom, and which would be laboring in the very *fire* for what is *but* vanity; and if ye will receive the knowledge which springs out of truth and life itself, which indeed flows over and covers the earth of God's heritage, as the waters cover the sea in this day of his *great* goodness and *plentiful* redemption.

" O what a day of mercy have we met with! and how great will be our condemnation, if we become as deaf adders to the Spirit of the Lord, and so miss our salvation. If we will know the Spirit of the Lord, we must *meet with him as a Searcher and Reprover in our hearts;* yea, the merciful God must we meet, as a severe Judge, and unquenchable, consuming fire, against *that* spirit, wisdom, knowledge, and faith in us, which is but of a *chaffy* nature. Truly, friends, it *is* far better to be *stripped* of it, than to find any rest or pleasure in it.

" It is of the infinite mercy and compassion of the Lord, that his pure love visiteth *any* of us; and, it is by the preservation thereof *alone,* that we stand. If he leave us at any time, but one moment, *what* are we? and *who* is there that provoketh Him not to depart? Let *him* throw the first stone at him that falls.

" In the truth itself, in the living power and virtue, there is *no offence;* but that part which is not perfectly redeemed hath still matter for temptation to work upon, and may be taken in the snare. Let him that stands take heed lest *he* fall; and in the bowels of pity mourn over and wait for the restoring of him that is fallen. *That which is so apt to be offended, is the same with that which falls.* Oh, do not reason in the high-mindedness against any that turn aside from the pure Guide; but *fear,* lest the *unbelieving and fleshly-wise* part get up in *thee* also. Oh, know the weakness of the creature in the withdrawings of life, and the strength of the mercy in *that* hour, and the free grace and mercy which alone can preserve! and thou wilt rather wonder that *any* stand, than that *some* fall.

"Oh, *great* is the mystery of Godliness, the way of life *narrow*, the travel to the land of rest *long, hard, and sharp ; it is easy miscarrying, it is easy stepping aside at any time ; it is easy losing the Lord's presence, unless the defence about it by his Almighty arm be kept up.* There is a time for the Lord's taking down the fence from his own vineyard, because of transgression, and then the wild boar may easily break in. Ah! *who* tastes not of this in some measure? and *what* hinders, that he tastes not of it in a *greater* measure?

"Ah, turn *from* the fleshly wisdom and reasonings *unto* the pure river of life itself, and wait there to have *that* judged which *hath taken offence,* lest, if it grow stronger in thee, it *draw* thee from the life which is alone able to preserve thee; and so, *thou* also fall! Retire from that part which *looketh out,* and feel the *inward* virtue of that which can restore and preserve thee."

Have we not long enough fed upon the fruit of the tree of outward knowledge, and seen enough of the evil of thus doing, to induce us to seek to turn to the tree of life which is in the midst of the paradise of God, the leaves of which *are* for the healing of the nations? Have we not seen sufficient of the fruit of fleshly wisdom, and the exercise thereof, to convince us of its alienating, dividing, and scattering power—of its *tendency* to destroy our unity with our Holy Head, and one with another, to induce us to forsake it, and *turn inward* to the secret and hidden life; to the word of faith which we preach, as our victory over the world?

Let us, individually, take these queries home to our own hearts, and still others, purposed by the Friend before referred to. "Hast thou known and experienced *Christ within,* redeeming thee from sin *within?* Hath Christ indeed brought salvation home to *thy own* heart? Hast thou known his inward and living power breaking the strength and power of Satan *within thee?* Hast thou known Him stronger than the strong man inwardly? Hast thou first known Christ knock at the door of thy heart, and opened to let him in, and afterwards experienced *what* he doth in the heart,

where he *is* let in ?   Or hast thou had only a *notional* knowledge
and belief concerning Christ *without*, and never known what it was
to have the Son *revealed in thee ?*   Hast thou only a *notion* of
Christ's blood as it was shed *without*, or dost thou also know the
sprinkling *within*, in thy own heart ?   Hath God made that new
covenant, the everlasting covenant with thee, wherein the blood of
sprinkling is felt, and the *precious effects of it experienced ?* for
then, indeed, iniquities are forgiven, and sin remembered no more ;
but the soul comes to witness *real* justification *from* sin, and *that*
peace which passeth understanding, which *no man* can give or take
away, neither doth any man know what it is but he that hath it.

"Deceit," saith he, "is very deep, and hath much prevailed.
There is a spirit of *delusion*, as well as of truth ; this works in the
heart as a minister of righteousness, in a *seeming* light, and warm-
ing the heart with a *wrong fire*, brings it into a *wrong bed* of rest,
and administers to it a *wrong peace, hope,* and *joy* ; setting up there
a *wrong sense, belief*, and *judgment concerning itself and others.*
This leads to *separate* from them that are *true*, and joins to them
that are *false*, and begets prejudices against, and hard thoughts of,
those who *are* owned by the Lord, and *are* kept in their habitation
by him who dwells in them, and they in him.

"Oh, dear friends ! *take heed of your own wisdom, your own
sense, your own judgment*, which you may easily through *mistake*
call the Lord's ; but to have all that is of self searched out and
brought under, and the mind made truly sensible of and fully *subject to the life* in everything,—this is sore travail ; and it is very
hard to come hither through all deceits and entanglements.   Take
heed of that which *prejudices* and *disjoins*, but feel and cleave to
that which *uniteth* in love, life, and pure power.   Know *that* unity
and fellowship which *is* in the Spirit, and keep it, keep in the bond
of pure peace ; and take heed, oh forever take heed of whatever
would break the bond ! but that which makes of *one* mind and one
judgment, one heart and one soul, *that is* the living principle, *that
is* the living power, which all the members of the body *are* to inha-
bit and be one in.   And watch against the *reasonings* of the mind,
and the thoughts of the heart, watch to the sense which riseth up
in the *fear*, in the *love*, in the *humility*, that you may feel the leadings of God's Spirit, and come through all that stands in your way,

having the help of all whom the Lord hath ordained and made able to be helpers.

"O! take heed of the *forwardness* of the flesh, the wisdom of the flesh, the will of the flesh, the talkativeness of the flesh. Keep them back. O! let *them* forever be kept back in every one of you by the presence and virtue of the power. Keep back to the life, keep low in the holy fear, and ye shall not miss of it. The power is the authority and blessing of your meetings, and therein lies your ability to perform what God requires. You will find it easy to transgress, easy to *set up self*, easy to run into *sudden apprehensions* about things, and one to be of *this* mind and another of *that;* but, feel the power to keep *down* all this, and to keep you *out* of all this; every one watching to the life, when and where it will arise to help you, and that ye may be made sensible of it when it doth arise, and not in a wrong wisdom oppose it, but be one with it. And thus, if anything should arise from the wrong wisdom in any, ye *may* be sensible of it, not defiled or entangled with it, but abiding in that which sees through it and judges it; that so life may reign in your hearts and in your meetings, above that which *will be forward and perking over the life,* if ye be not watchful. Then all that is evil and contrary to Truth, being kept down in *your own* hearts, ye will be fit to keep down evil in the minds and hearts of *others;* and, if anything be unsavory anywhere, it will be searched out, judged, cast out, and the *recovery of the soul which hath let it in, sought,* that, if possible, it may be restored; and then ye will know the joy of *seeking out and bringing back the lost sheep.*

"Be *tender* to others, in the true compassion, as ye would be tendered by others, if ye were in their condition. If at any time ye have anything against others, O, learn from that of God in you, to show compassion towards them, even as the Lord hath had pity on you! Have you somewhat against others whereupon you forbear meeting with them? Is the thing, or *are* the things which you have against them, fully so, as you apprehend? Have you *seen* evil in them, or to break forth from them? and have you considered *them* therein, and dealt with them as if it had been your own case? *Have you pitied them, mourned over them, cried unto the Lord for them, and in tender love and meekness of spirit laid the thing before them?* And, if they have refused to hear you, have you ten-

*derly* mentioned it to others and desired them to go with you to them, that what is evil and offensive in them might be more weightily and advantageously laid before them for their humbling, and for their *recovery* unto that, which is a witness and strength against the evil? If you have proceeded thus, you have proceeded tenderly and orderly, according to the law of brotherly love, and God's witness in your consciences *will* justify you therein. But, if you let in any hardness of spirit, or hard reasonings against them, or hard resolutions as relating to them, the witness for God will *not* justify you in that."

Now, how hath it been with us in this day of offence and taking offence, because of those things permitted for the trial of our faith and patience? Have we proceeded, in all things, according to Gospel order, and in the spirit of meekness and love, seeking the *recovery* of the erring? or have we not, through the prevalence of evil in our own hearts, indulged the spirit of the accuser, which was so emphatically rebuked by our holy Redeemer, in the case of one taken in the very act of offence? O, let us remember, for our instruction and encouragement, in the right way, the wise and faithful reply made to the accusers of the offender, by which she was acquitted of them and *left alone with the blessed Master.* "*Let him that is without sin cast the first stone.*"

O, how much of the contention and strife by which our true peace and enjoyment have been disturbed, how much of the trouble, perplexity, and confusion which we have suffered, might have been, and may still be avoided, by attention to the precepts of our holy Redeemer and the *gentle* leadings of his Holy Spirit! by which we are taught the exercise of forbearance and forgiveness, even toward our outward enemies, seeking to *restore* the erring in the spirit of meekness, remembering ourselves lest we also be tempted. O, how have the leaders of the people caused them to err, through the countenance and encouragement of the spirit of accusation and fault-finding, by which it has been made to appear, to the unwary mind, that the religion of Jesus Christ consists in watching for and exposing the faults of the brethren!

But the time *hath come* when the evil of an error so fatal to the peace and harmony of the Church is being more clearly seen, and more faithfully testified against; wherefore we may look for the increase of Gospel unity and fellowship amongst us, through the prevalence of that love and order which marks the advancement of the blessed cause, the coming of the kingdom of Christ in our hearts, that the will of God may be done therein, as it is done in heaven, where all jarring and contention, enmity and discord, are forever excluded, and the reign of harmony, love, and joy are eternally known to prevail, to the glory of Him who sitteth upon the throne, receiving the praises and hallelujahs of the redeemed, who have been *washed* in the blood of the Lamb, and are clothed in *white* raiment, with the palms of victory in their hands.

O, the blessedness of that state, wherein we are permitted to have a little foretaste of the eternal joys of heaven, wherein we experience the coming of the kingdom of our God, and the power of his Christ in our hearts, *casting down the accuser of the brethren* and establishing the reign of righteousness and peace! What can we desire in comparison with this? and how can we knowingly and wilfully do anything to frustrate this gracious end, as it respects ourselves and others, whom the Lord, in his unspeakable and unmerited mercy, *is* seeking to gather *out* of the world and its spirit *into* the life and peace which shall never end?

O, that we were wise, that we would more often and constantly consider the end of our creation and being! that we might experience that enlargement of heart which would enable us to own all who are owned by Him who is the Father of us all, as it respects our creation, and whose children, by adoption, are all those who are engaged in the performance and suffering of his holy will; that we might know the fortification of our minds against all straightness, bigotry, and self-righteousness, whereby our hearts are corrupted as by the leaven of the Pharisees—by the spirit of party—whereby we are separated from union and communion with Christ and his true followers.

"The Scribes and Pharisees," saith I. P., "who were interpreters of the law, and very strict in outward observances, ordinances, &c., who blamed their fathers for killing the prophets, and said, if they had been in the days of the prophets, they would not have dealt so with them as their fathers did; yet, concerning these said Stephen, ' *Ye stiff-necked and uncircumcised in heart and ears, ye do also resist the Holy Ghost; as your fathers did, so do ye;*' for, till *the stiff will, and stiff wisdom* be brought down in a man, he cannot but resist God's Spirit, and fight for *his* notions and practices, according to *his* apprehensions of the letter, *against* the testimony of God's Spirit and power.

"Paul, who walked according to the letter of the law, blameless, yet resisted the Spirit which gave forth the law. He must know the Spirit, receive the Spirit, walk in the Spirit, and not fulfil the lusts of the flesh, who would not be found resisting God's Spirit. He is, indeed, turned to the redeeming arm, to Christ the power of God, and gathered into the power, and dwelleth in the Spirit and power of the Lord Jesus, and is taught and led by him from path to path, and from pasture to pasture, as the Lamb, the Shepherd *goes before* and *guides* him; he *is* preserved from *grieving* the Holy Spirit, which moves and draws, instructs and quickens, all that *are* born of God. But he that is only in the *letter* and in the *form* of godliness, out of the inward life and power, he is of *that* birth, mind, nature, and spirit which cannot but resist God's Spirit. He knoweth not, he heedeth not his drawings, his movings, his light, his life, the way thereof, either in his own heart or in the hearts of others, and so walks in a way of rebelling against and resisting Him who is the only Saviour and Redeemer of the soul." See Job 29 : 3, 4, and 24 : 13.

"Come, O, come to the true root! Come to Christ, indeed! But not in an *outward knowledge*, but come to the *inward life*, the hidden life, and receive life from Him who is the life; and then abide in and live *to* him in the life of his Son; for death and destruction, corruption and vanity, *may* talk of the fame of Christ, who is the wisdom of God; but they *cannot* know nor find out the place where this wisdom is revealed; they cannot come at the true, pure fear, which God puts into the hearts of *his;* this is the beginning of *true* wisdom, which cleanses darkness and impurity out of the hearts of those to whom it is given. Christ, where he is received, bindeth and casts out the strong man taking possession of the heart. And if any be truly and really in Christ, he comes to witness a new creation, even the passing away of old things, and all things become new. What shall become of those that do not fight *under* Christ?" Read Rev. 3 : 21.

"Alas! men building in the flesh, after the carnal apprehension of things,—how *loathsome* is it! but God's building, raised in the light and life of his pure Spirit, how *glorious*, how *beautiful*, how *lovely* is it, even in the eye of God himself! 'Thou art fair, my

love, there is no spot in thee.' Into thy heavenly building, O
God! into the spiritual Jerusalem, which thou rearest and buildest
up in the Spirit, *no* unclean nor defiled thing can enter; nor is
there any place there for that which loves and makes a lie! Without, indeed, are swine and dogs, vulturous eyes and crooked ser-
pents, who make a show of what they are not, and lay claim to
that which belongs not to them; but *within* are the children, *within*
is the heavenly birth, even the new creature of God in Christ
Jesus.

" O, what becomes of flesh, and self, and *self-righteousness* when
the seed lives in the heart! there Christ is formed, of a truth, and
the *black* garments of unrighteousness, yea, of *man's* righteousness
too, are put off, and the *white* raiment put on; here the holy image
is brought forth in the heart, even the image of the dear Son, which
partakes of the *divine* nature of the Father; here, is *no deceit of
any kind* met with, but only *truth* from God, even the true life,
light, virtue, power, of the Lord Jesus as livingly felt in the heart,
as effectually operating there as ever the power of sin did.

" The Apostle speaks of the Gentiles before they were turned
from darkness to light, and from the power of Satan to God, that
their understanding was *darkened*, being alienated from the life of
God, *because of the hardness of their hearts;* not that that which
might be known of God was not manifest in them, but their ignorance was because of their hardness *in not minding it*, not turning
to it, and so they became alienated from the life, and their understanding *not* opened to it.

" Now, in this state, men *are* without God, without Christ, stran-
gers to the covenant of promise, and without any *true* hope of salvation; and this state they are as really in, who get a *form* of
Godliness *without* the power, as the very natural heathen; for
nothing makes a *true* Christian, but the life and power, and he that
doth not hear the voice of Christ's Spirit in *his* heart, is no better
than a heathen and a publican. They that say they are Jews, but
are *not* so; ministers of Christ, but are not so, and do lie; alas!
what are they? Indeed, the nakedness of such as are not clothed
with God's Spirit doth appear to the Lord, and to the eyes and
spirits of *his* children which he openeth in *his own* light, and who
see with *this* eye;—I say the shame of their nakedness *doth* appear, notwithstanding all the religious covers they can put upon
themselves.

"Oh learn to distinguish between words *without concerning* the thing, and *the thing itself within*, and wait and labor then to know, understand, and be guided by, the motives, leadings, drawings, teachings, quickenings, etc., of the thing itself *within*. And *take heed of being offended because of anything either within or without*, for offences will come, but blessed *was* he that *was not* offended at Christ outwardly, in the days of his flesh; and blessed *is* he that *is not* offended at his *inward* Truth and inward way of appearance in the day of his Spirit. Moses, that precious servant of the Lord, spake *unadvisedly* with his lips: how easy is it, then, for those who come not near Moses's state to do so. Wait on God, that ye may distinguish between what *Truth speaks inwardly*, and what *any of us may unadvisedly speak out of the Truth*, if we stand not upon the watch and our words be *not seasoned* with God's light, and his grace. Take heed of mistaking the testimony in any, or of being stumbled if any go *beyond* their due bounds in their testimony.

"Oh desire to be good, upright, and perfect in God's sight, and *wait to feel the life, Spirit, and power which makes so.* Come ye out of the knowledge and comprehension *about* things, into the *feeling life*, and let *that* be your knowledge and wisdom, which is received and retained in the feeling life, and that will lead into the footsteps of the flock *without* reasoning, consulting, or disputing. Oh wait to be taught and enabled by God to fetch *right* steps in your travels, and to take up the cross and despise the shame in everything wherein *that* wisdom, will, and mind, which *is* to be crucified, *would* be judge, for it *will* judge amiss, and lead aside if it be hearkened to.

"We must be very low, weak, and foolish, that the seed may arise in us to exalt us, and become our strength and wisdom; and we must die exceedingly, again and again, more and more, inwardly and deeply! that our life may spring up from the holy root and stock, and we be more and more gathered into it, spring up into it, and live *alone* in the life, virtue, and power thereof. The travel is long, the snares, temptations, and dangers many, and yet the mercy, relief, and help is great also. O, that ye may be led into the *true subjection*, which brings forth the true dominion! that in *one* virtue and power of life we may be *knit together* and serve the Lord in perfect unity of spirit."

In this subjection, dominion, and unity, is our strength to suffer, as well as to perform the will of our Holy Head—to answer the blessed end of our calling, even the praise and honor of Him who created us for the purpose of his own glory, and with an outstretched arm gathered our worthy forefathers out of the world and its spirit, into the unity and fellowship of the Gospel, enabling them to bear a united and faithful testimony against the customs, fashions, and practices of those who are unredeemed from the earthly spirit and wisdom, whereby they are led into contention and strife, jarring and discord, dissensions and divisions, wars and fightings, tyranny and oppression, and many other temptations and evils against which every true friend of Truth is bound to bear testimony.

How, then, can any assert or believe that the Society of Friends has accomplished its mission, while there still exists in the earth, and even amongst ourselves, such an abundance of the evils which it was raised up to testify against—while wars and fightings, oppression and violence, sin and corruption, are still known in the world, and idolatry and priestcraft, superstition and bigotry, time-serving and worldly-mindedness in the Church, to the abridgment of the natural and religious rights of our fellows, and the disturbance of the peace and harmony of society? How can we submit to the invasion of the spirit of faction and separation, allowing it to triumph over the Spirit of Truth in our hearts, to the alienation of them from the pure and peaceable principle of Gospel love, by which we profess to be influenced and governed, without surrendering our claim to the name we bear, and incurring the displeasure of Him whom we profess to worship and serve?

O, let us examine ourselves in the undeceiving light of Truth, that we may be enabled to search and cast out the unholy spirit which is breaking our ranks, and threatening to disband the armies of Israel, lest we become hopelessly scattered, even as the favored people of old, who despised and rejected the Son and sent of God, because of the meanness and lowness of his outward appearance amongst them. As it is written, "He came unto his own, but his own received him not." And may not the same testimony apply unto many in this day, respecting his spiritual and inward appearance? Has not this been despised and rejected, because of its smallness; and the spirit, will, and wisdom of self exalted in our hearts, to the crucifying afresh of the dear Son of God, putting him to an open shame, through submitting to the usurpation of his proper dominion and reign, by the power and prince of the air?

O, let us seek once more to rally to the standard of Truth, laying aside the armor of Saul, and putting on the armor of light, going forth in the authority and power of the living and eternal truth, against the disturber and defier of Israel, who is seeking to destroy our faith in that which giveth the victory over death and darkness, and prepareth for the enjoyment of the incorruptible, undefiled, and unfading inheritance which is promised to all them that are sanctified and justified by the washing of regeneration and renewing of the Holy Ghost.

The Lord *is* still waiting to be gracious, and will again extend his restoring and gathering arm of mercy and power, for our strength and help, in the work of redemption and salvation, as we are engaged to walk in *fear and trembling* before him, and in *all lowliness and uprightness* to promote his honor and glory, through the advancement of his blessed cause in the earth—the hastening of the coming, and spread of his holy and heavenly kingdom—until righteousness shall cover the earth as the waters do the sea, until swords shall be beaten into ploughshares, and spears into pruning hooks, and men shall learn war no more; until the lion and the lamb shall lie down together, and all enmity shall be destroyed by the power of the living seed and word of God; and the establishment of righteousness and peace be known throughout the earth.

As it was for the hastening of the coming of this blessed and holy state of harmony and peace that our worthy forefathers in the Truth—that the holy Apostles and those who have succeeded them in the espousal of the cause of spiritual religion—were called out of the world and its spirit, to testify against the works of darkness, to "turn men from darkness to light, and from the power of Satan unto God," O, how does it behoove us not to frustrate the grace and goodness of God, by hindering or preventing his gracious design, through the letting in of those evil propensities of our unrenewed nature, by which we are led to indulge the corrupting and limiting spirit, the unholy leaven of party, either in our ministry, or the administration of the discipline of the church, lest we continue to be scattered, and have sorrow upon sorrow.

Of what an ill and unholy savor is that *bitterness* of spirit by which we are led into wranglings and disputings about those things which should be settled according to the order and direction of Truth, as prescribed by the precepts of Holy Writ, and the corresponding injunctions of our Christian discipline. And where shall we land, but in anarchy and confusion, if we allow these to be trampled under foot at the pleasure, and for the gratification of the creaturely will,—for the purpose of answering party ends? Shall we not be brought under the condemnation of the Scribes and Pharisees, by attending to the suggestions of our own wills and wisdom, while we neglect the weightier matters of the law?

O, may we not confidently hope that the time is approaching, and near at hand, when through the mighty judgments of the Most High, we shall be brought to see and acknowledge the error of perverting the end of our religious association, by seeking to close up the way for the mutual exercise of those gifts which have been bestowed upon us for the edification of the body in love—when we shall again be brought together in the unity of the faith of Christ, which is our victory over the world, unto " the unity of the Spirit in the bond of peace?"

What but the pride, will, and prejudice,—but the corruption of our own hearts—hath divided, and is keeping asunder, those who are professing the same principles, the same faith, and the support of the same testimonies? and what but the laying aside, the purging out of these, is needed to bring us together again under the *one holy banner of Christian love and unity?* O, the fault *is* our own, and we must correct it, through the holy help which is graciously offered and extended for our *deliverance from the sin and iniquity of our own hearts;* for the Lord will be merciful to our unrighteousness and remember our sins and iniquities no more, if we will only be persuaded to turn our backs upon those things which are standing in our way to unity with Christ, and one with another—that are separating our hearts from union and communion with the Father, through his well beloved Son—the Lamb of God, who taketh away the sins of the world—and preventing us from journeying forward harmoniously together, to the promised land of rest and peace.

" We are here but a little while in this world," saith I. P., " for the Lord to make use of us, and serve himself by us; and so by *his* ordering of us, to fit us for the crown of glory which he will give us fully to wear in the other world. O, feel the child's nature which *chooseth nothing*, but desires the fulfilling of the Father's will in it. O, at all times, and in all conditions *take heed of a will, take heed of a wisdom, above the seed's will, and above the seed's wisdom!* The error is still in the comprehending, knowing mind, but never in the lowly weighty seed of life. The greatest as well as the least, must be *daily* taught of the Lord, both in ascending and descending, or they will miss their way; yea, they must be daily taught of him to be silent before him, and know what it is to be *still in him*, or they will be apt to miss in either.

"Ah! that wisdom which would be choosing must be confounded, and the *low humble thing* raised, which *submits* without murmuring, and cries to the Father in every condition. Israel of old, after the flesh, murmured upon every trial; but Israel of the new creation, doeth *not* so, but blesseth the Lord, and repineth not at the instruments which he permitteth to afflict them; but they love the Lord, and love his truth, and are faithful in their testimony thereto, whatever befalls them. Yea, they rejoice that they are counted worthy to suffer in any kind for his name's sake, and are like lambs before the shearers, *not* opening their mouths in a way of *murmuring or reviling*, but instead thereof pitying them, praying for them, and blessing; because God hath made them children of love, *children of peace, children of blessing;* which nature they retain in the midst of all their trials and afflictions, and show forth the virtues of Him that hath called them.

"The spirits of those who dwell in the *fear and dread* of the Lord God Almighty are much raised, and the fear and dread of man is removed far away. Lo, I come, saith the child, to do thy will, O God! to drink the cup thou hast prepared; although there is a nature which cannot but say, If it be possible let it pass away; but, *that* nature is bowed down and subjected under its proper yoke, and, in submission, is kept out of sinning against the Lord, and is accepted by him who bows it, and makes it willing to follow the Lamb in the day of his power, so that it shall not put out our life, nor put out our light, nor *sever us from the love and power of God;* but the more need we find of our God, and of his help and strength, the nearer shall we be driven to him, and dwell more closely in unity with him, and in holy and humble dependence upon him. And, in *this* temper, shall we draw and receive more from him; and the more we draw from him the better will it be with us, and the more *like him* shall we be.

· "The Lord keep open that heavenly eye in his children and servants, which looks over this world, with the affairs and concerns thereof, to that which *is* immortal and invisible, where *our life is hid from others*, though made manifest in and felt by us from the living spring which quickens, nourisheth, and refresheth. And as afflictions abound from men, so shall consolation, life, and strength abound from the Lord unto all and upon all who *look not out*, but abide and await there where it springs and flows. O, my Friends, *look not out* at what stands in the way; what if it look dreadfully as a lion, *is not the Lord stronger than the mountains of prey?* Look *in* where the law of life is written, and the will of the Lord revealed, that the will of the Lord concerning you may be known; and then show yourselves the faithful children of Abraham, and be like Sarah, not terrified with any amazement.

"The more the spirit is broken by the hand of the Lord, and taught thereby to fear him, and the less strength it hath in itself to grapple with the persecuting spirit of the world, the fitter it is to stand in God's counsel, to wait for his strength and preservation, which is able to bear up its head above all the rage and swelling of the waters of the worldly spirit in the men of this world."

Thus was this meek and humble servant of the Lord Jesus Christ moved to write for the encouragement and comfort of the tribulated followers of the Lamb of God; and in addressing their persecutors, he used the following significant language, unto which we shall all do well to take heed in this day of suffering from the oppression of the enemy; who, like a roaring lion, is seeking to destroy and devour the heritage of God, by raising up the spirit of persecution within our own borders.

"As the Lord is able to overturn you, so if ye mistake your work, misinterpreting the passages of his providence, and erring in heart concerning the ground of his former displeasure; and so, (through the error of judgment) set yourselves in opposition against him, do ye not provoke the Lord, even to put forth the strength which is in him against you? We are poor worms. Alas! if ye had only us to deal with, we should be as nothing in your hands! But if his strength stand behind us, we shall prove ● very burdensome stone, and ye will hardly be able to remove us out of the place wherein God has set us, and where he pleaseth to have us disposed of. And happy were it for you, if instead of persecuting us, ye

yourselves were drawn to wait for the same begettings of God
(which we have felt) out of the *earthly* nature, into *his* life and
nature, and did learn of him to govern in *that;* then might ye be
established indeed, and be freed from the danger of those shakings
and overturnings which God is hastening upon the earth.

" Now because ye may be apt to think that I write these things
for my own sake, and the sake of my friends and companions in the
truth of God, that we might escape the sufferings and severity
which we are like to undergo from you, and not so mainly and
chiefly for your sakes, lest ye should bring the wrath of God and
misery upon your souls and bodies; to prevent this mistake in you,
I shall add what followeth. Indeed, this is not the intent of my
heart, for I have long expected, and do still expect, this cup of
outward affliction and persecution from you, and my heart is quieted
and satisfied therein, knowing that the Lord *will* bring glory to *his*
*name*, and good to *us* out of it; but I am sure it is *not* good for
*you*, to afflict us for that which the Lord requireth of us, and ye
will find it the bitterest work that ever ye went about, and in the
end will wish the Lord had rather never given you this day of prosperity, than that he should have suffered you *thus* to make use
of it. * * * *

" The strength of man, the resolution of man, is nothing in my
eye, in comparison with the Lord. Whom *he* loveth, he can save
at his pleasure. Are we in a worse condition than Israel was, when
the sea was before them, the mountains on each side, and the
Egyptians behind pursuing them ? He, indeed, that looketh with
man's eye, can see no ground of hope, nor hardly a possibility of
deliverance; but (to the eye of faith) it is now nearer than when
God first began to deliver.

" It is the delight of the Lord, and his glory, to deliver his people
when, to the eye of sense, it seems impossible. Then doth the Lord
delight to stretch forth his arm, when none else can help; and then
doth it please him to deal with the enemies of his truth and people,
when they are lifted up above the fear of him, and are ready to say
in their hearts concerning them: They are now in our hands, who
can deliver them ?

" Well, were it not in love to you, and in pity (in relation to what
will *certainly* befall you, if ye go on in this course), I could say in the
joy of my heart, and in the sense of the good-will of God to us, who

suffereth these things to come to pass, Go on; try it out with the Spirit of the Lord. Come forth with your [persecutions] and banishment, and (if the Lord please) see if ye can carry it; for we come not forth against you in our own wills, or in any enmity against your persons, or in any stubbornness or refractiousness of spirit, *but with the Lamb-like nature*, which the Lord our God hath begotten in us, which is taught and enabled by him, both to do his will, and to suffer for his name's sake. And if we cannot thus overcome you (even in patience of spirit and in love to you), and if the Lord our God please not appear for us, we are content to be overcome by you. So the will of the Lord be done, saith my soul."

Says the editor of the work from which this last extract is taken: "While the preceding paragraphs exhibit an unshaken confidence in Divine support, and a Christian firmness in pleading the cause of religious liberty, rarely surpassed; the following extract from a piece, which appears to have been written about the same time, evinces that the author *possessed,* in an eminent degree, that charity, the absence of which *no other* Christian virtue can supply." And it may be added, that it evinces a sense of the universality of Divine grace, by which we are delivered from that straitness and bigotry which would be limiting the visitations, workings, and power thereof within the narrow boundary of human comprehension.

Saith he, "My soul hath mourned, I may say, almost from my cradle, about the estate of *this creation.* To behold man fallen from his glory, departed from his God, living without the sense of him, and sowing the seeds of eternal misery for his poor soul (which he must as certainly reap as he hath sown, unless he travel the path of redemption in the powerful leadings and guidance of God's Holy Spirit): this hath so broken my heart (together with the close exercises which have continually attended this poor wearied spirit), that I have often wondered how the natural life could be contained in the natural vessel.

"I am a *lover of mankind in general,* and have been a deep sufferer with, and travailler for *all the miserable.* None knows the path of my sorrows, or *the extent of my bowels,* but he that made me. It is not natural or kindly to me to upbraid any man with any kind of wickedness or ever so justly deserved misery, but my bowels work concerning him towards the Spring of eternal power and compassions, *even as I would be pitied and represented to the Father of mercies in the like condition.* Indeed I have been emptied from vessel to vessel, and tossed with multitudes of storms and tempests, yet the savor of my life remaineth with me to this day, and the Spirit of my God breatheth on my heart: blessed be his Holy Name for ever.

" And though I walk with one sort of people, because my heart saith that they are the people whom God hath chosen out of all the gatherings (throughout the earth) from this apostacy, to manifest his power in, and his presence among; I say, though I have been guided by the Spirit of the Lord to walk among those, *yet I am not bounded there, either in the love or in the unity of my heart, but I have unity with the integrity and zeal for God which is in others, of what sort or gathering soever; and I have tender bowels for all, even for those which hate and persecute that which is my life, and hath the love of my heart forever.*

" Oh! how have I prayed for *the lost world! For all the souls of mankind,* how hath my soul bowed in unutterable breathings of spirit before God, and could not be silenced until he quieted my spirit in the righteousness and excellency of his will, and bid me *leave it to him.* And as touching this nation, and the several sorts in it, *even those who seem most cast off,* and without all sense (religious sensibility); yet the preciousness of *their* souls have I spread before the Lord my God with tears."

The following is part of an address by I. P. to people of *several different classes. " To such as are still tender, and dare not but exercise a conscience towards God.* Friends, keep your standing in the life of God. Let the tenderness of your consciences, which is of value with God, be precious in your eyes. The times and seasons *are* in the Father's hand, and he seeth good to let this day of trial come upon you. His grace is able to carry *you all* through. It will be for his honor to let all the world see how dear your God is to you, and how able ye are (in the meekness and strength of the Lamb's Spirit) to suffer for his name's sake. Thy will, O Lord, be done. The cup which our Father gives us, shall we not drink it? The Lord preserve you in uprightness of heart towards him, *in meekness of spirit toward those that afflict you, and in true love and good-will towards all,* that his light which hath gathered you may shine over all the darkness which opposeth it, and his life which both quickened and preserved you, may be famous over all the territories and dominions of death."

What an evidence of enlargement of heart is to be found in this and much that precedeth it! and how desirable is it for us to press toward this "mark for the prize of the high calling of God in Christ Jesus," even the unbounded love of the Gospel which was begotten in the heart of the Apostle of the Gentiles—after he had been redeemed from the righteousness of self, in which he was led to persecute the Church of Christ—when he was moved to declare his thankfulness for his recovery from ignorance and unbelief; "who," said he, "was before a blasphemer, and a persecutor, and injurious; but I obtained mercy, because I did it ignorantly in unbelief."

In renouncing his confidence in the flesh, he says, "What things *were* gain to me, these I counted loss for Christ, and do count them *but* dung that I may win Christ and be found in him, not having on *my own* righteousness, which is of the law, but that which is through the faith of Christ." Then was he made sensible of the inestimable value of the love of God which had been shed abroad in his heart, purging it of that straitness and bigotry, whereby he had been held in bondage to the spirit of the world, and led to believe that in persecuting the Church he was doing God service. Then was he led to declare, that though he spake with the tongues of men and of angels, and had not charity, he was become as sounding brass or a tinkling cymbal; and though he had the gift of prophecy, and understood all mysteries and all knowledge—and though he had all faith, so that he could remove mountains—and had not charity, he was nothing.

And of this Divine and indispensable virtue, he testified, no doubt from living experience, that it "suffereth *long* and is kind, envieth not, vaunteth not itself, is not puffed up, doth not behave itself unseemly, seeketh not her own, is not easily provoked, thinketh no evil, rejoiceth not in iniquity, but rejoiceth in the truth; beareth all things, believeth all things, hopeth all things, endureth all things, and never faileth." Is not this a pearl of great price? in the possession of which is known a measure of that peace which the world can neither give nor take away—the perfection of which passeth all human understanding!

But, O! the sacrifices and sufferings of those who are brought into the possession of it, how many and how great they are! How much have we to part with and to endure, before we can attain to the pure love of God which breatheth peace on earth and good-will to men, casting down all the high thoughts and lofty imaginations, whereby self is exalted above the little pure witness for God in our souls, and we are made to esteem ourselves better than others. O, the allurements and deceit of the Evil One, who caused our first parents to violate the Divine command, whereby they were driven out of the paradise of God; how are they still working in order to rob us of our crown! How is the spirit of deceit seeking to lead us into rebellion against God, who hath set a hedge about us, and planted within the sacred inclosure the Tree of Life!

But blessed be the God of Israel, who hath ever wrought deliverance for his people, he hath declared through his prophet, "I am against thee, Pharaoh, king of Egypt, the great dragon that lieth in the midst of his rivers, which hath said, My river is *mine own*, and I have made it for myself. But I will put hooks in thy jaws, and I will cause the fish of thy rivers to stick unto thy scales; and I will bring thee up out of the midst of thy rivers, and all the fish of thy rivers shall stick into thy scales; and I will leave thee thrown into the wilderness, thee and all the fish of thy rivers; thou shalt fall upon the open fields; thou shalt not be brought together nor gathered; I have given thee for meat to the beasts of the field and to the fowls of heaven. And all the inhabitants of Egypt shall know that I am the Lord, because they have been a staff of reed to the house of Israel. When they took hold of thee by the hand thou didst break and rend all their shoulder; and when they leaned upon thee thou breakest and madest all their loins at a stand. Therefore, saith the Lord God, Behold, I will bring a sword upon thee, and cut off man and beast out of thee, and the land of Egypt shall be desolate and waste; and they shall know that I *am* the Lord; because he hath said, *The river is mine, and I have made it.*"

This is to be the end of self-exaltation, and happy will it be for those who are not corrupted or defiled thereby, or have not, in the exaltation of their hearts against the Lord and his truth, been the means of causing others to lean on the broken reed of self-righteousness. "Who shall ascend into the hill of the Lord? and who shall stand in his holy place? He that hath clean hands and a pure héart; who hath *not lifted up his soul unto vanity, nor sworn deceitfully*. He shall receive blessing from the Lord, and righteousness from the God of his salvation."

Concerning *selfish wisdom*, self-exaltation, and deceit and their opposites, Isaac Penington bears the following testimony: "Every step of thy way the selfish wisdom will be laying baits for thee, and it is easy for *deceit* to enter thee at any time, and for that wisdom to get up in thee *under an appearance of spiritual wisdom*, unless the Lord tenderly and powerfully preserve thee; and if it prevail it will lead thee from the path of the true wisdom, it will cozen thee with a *false* faith, instead of the true faith; with diligence and zeal in thy false way, instead of the true zeal and diligence; yea, it will hurry thee on in the path of error, shutting *that eye* in thee which should see, and hardening thy heart against thy bosom friend; and being thus deceived, thou mayest be as zealous in thy age and generation against the truth as the Jews were in theirs; and as certainly as they put Christ to death, and persecuted his Apostles, though they cried up the former prophets, so certainly thou (under this deceit) *canst not but* act against the present dispensation and appearance of Christ's Spirit, and wouldst persecute either the prophets, Apostles, or Christ himself, if their present day were now, so to appear as formerly they did.

"The powers of darkness are continually at hand, which nothing can stand its ground against (much less walk on safely) without being in the power which is above them. Ye must be clothed with the Spirit, clothed with the *Lamb's* righteousness, and thus ye must appear before the Lord in his temple, where ye are never to appear in your own filthy rags, but in the nature, Spirit, righteousness, and life of Christ. And thus ye are well pleasing to God even in *that* which is of God, being born of that, formed of that, found in that, appearing in that. But in *his own*, no man can be accepted; for it is determined of God, and stands irreversible forever, that in his own (in his own knowledge, in his own faith, in his own obedience, in his own righteousness, in his own willing and running, &c.), shall no flesh ever be justified in his sight.

"The man who is not born of the Spirit, but pretends to be of this birth from above, runs into inventions and imaginations, and sets up a way of his own choosing, which he having much considered of, and beat out by reasonings, and fenced about with arguments, he grows wise in his own eyes, and now verily believes it to be the way of God, and that he is able to maintain it against all opposers. But oh! that where there is any true honest upright desire after God, from the simplicity of the heart, it might not be *thus* betrayed through the subtilty of the fleshly wisdom, which lies lurking in the wise, reasoning, knowing part, to *betray the poor weak babe.* The natural man, the wise man, according to the natural wisdom, cannot understand the things of God.

"There is that which deceives where it is hearkened to, and there is that which is liable to be deceived by it. There is likewise that which deceiveth not, and there is also that which cannot be deceived. So likewise there is a pure fear and watching in the truth against the deceit, lest by any means it should enter and betray. Who is it, at this day, who escapeth the snare of calling evil good, and good evil? Surely none but he whose soul is led into, and lives in, the light and power of truth. As there is one that *gathers* to the true Church, so there is another that endeavors to draw and scatter from it, and then to cause man to turn head against it, as if it were not of God, but apostatized from the Spirit and principle of truth, which is indeed their own state and condition in God's sight."

In reference to the order and government of the Church of Christ, Isaac Penington bears the following testimony. "It is not an *easy* matter, in all cases, clearly and understandingly to discern the voice of the Shepherd, the motion of God's Spirit, and yet there is a preservation to that which is *lowly and submissive*, looking up to the Lord continually, and not trusting to *its own* understanding, sense, and judgment. But that which is *hasty and confident*, and so *ready to plead its own sense and judgment* according to the measure of life, *as it calls it;* that is commonly out, entered into the erring spirit, pleading and contending for it knows not what, and is very apt to judge and condemn others in that very respect, wherein itself is most justly and righteously judged and condemned by the Lord, even by his pure life and Spirit in his people.

"Let the [true] measure of life judge freely in thee concerning anything, and that judgment shall stand forever. But be thou wary, wait on the Lord that thou mayst *be sure* thou dost not mistake in thy own particular, calling that life which the Lord and his people know to be otherwise; for if so, thou departest from the unity and bond of the Spirit, and from the true sense and judgment, and givest deceit an advantage over thee, even to lay a foundation of destroying thee. Likewise those who are to watch over thee in the Lord—to lay his truth before thee, to exhort and reprove thee, as occasion is—that. they may give an account of thy soul to him, cannot do it with joy and rejoicing in his presence, but with grief and lamentation of heart, which is not at all profitable, but very unprofitable for thee.

"A watch is to be kept, throughout the whole body and in every heart, for the preservation of unity, so far as it is brought forth, that the enemy, by no device or subtilty, cause disunion or difference in any respect, wherein there was once a true unity and oneness; for the enemy *will watch to divide;* and if he is not watched against in that which is able to discover and keep him out, by some device or other he will take his advantage to make a rent in those that are not watchful, from the pure truth and unity of life in the body; for he that in the least thing rents from the body, he in that respect hearkens to another spirit, even *the dividing spirit,* and by its instigation rents from the life itself, and so doth not keep his habitation, nor his unity, with that which abides in its habitation.

"Tenderness, meekness, coolness, and stillness of spirit are of a uniting, preserving nature. He that differs and divides from the body *cannot* be thus; and he that is thus *cannot* rend or divide. This is the pure heavenly wisdom which is peaceable and keepeth the peace; but the *other* wisdom is rough, stiff, hard, clamorous, ready to take offence, ready to give offence; exceeding deep in the justification of *itself*, exceeding deep in the condemnation of *others,* and dares, in this temper, appeal to the Lord, as if it were right in its ways, but wronged by others; as if it did abide in the measure of truth and life which others have departed from. And how can it be otherwise? How can the wrong eye, the wrong spirit, the wrong wisdom, but judge wrong, justifying the wrong practices, and condemning the right? But such shall find (if they come to the true touchstone, even the measure of life indeed) that they are *not* in the true tenderness which proceeds from the life, in the true meekness and gentleness, in the true coolness and stillness; but rather in the reasonings, noises, clamors, and disturbances which arise from *another* spirit, mind, and nature than that which *is* of the truth. And in coming back from *this* wisdom, to the *pure* wisdom, from the

*pretended* measure of life to the *true* measure, and becoming tender, meek, cool, and still on it, they shall feel their error from the
Spirit and power of the Lord, and therein own their condemnation
therefor from him, and also justify them who have abode in the
power and been guided by the Spirit and pure measure of life which
*is* from God, and in God, while they have departed from it; for
the spirit of error wherewith they have been deceived and entangled, hath made them believe that *they* have faithfully abode in the
principle and doctrine of truth, while *others* have departed, yet
that will soon vanish, as truth comes to be felt and heard speak in
them, and the measure of life to live in them, and to redeem them
into its holy nature and pure living sense.

" He that is tempted, he that often falls, and is so often wounded
and made miserable, he *pities* those that err, he mourns over the
miserable. His heart is broken with the sins and afflictions of
others, and he knoweth not how to be hard towards them, feeling
*such need* of continual mercy himself. It is the rich man, the
sound man in religion, that is rough and hard; but he that *is* once
thoroughly melted in the furnace and made up again, is made but
tender, and retaineth the impression of the meekness, love, and
mercy forever. Now, a *broken* estate in religion, or a state of waiting for the life is much more precious than that which is *rich* and
*full* by what it had formerly received, and still holdeth *out of the
immediate and fresh virtue of life.*

" The enemy is very subtle and watchful, and there is danger to
Israel all along, both in the poverty and in the riches; but the
greater danger in the riches, because *then* man is apt to forget God,
and to lose somewhat of the sense of dependence (which keeps the
soul *low and safe* in the life), and also to suffer somewhat of *exaltation* to creep upon him, which presently, in a degree, *corrupts* and
*betrays* him. *The heart that is in any measure lifted up in itself,
so far it is not upright in the Lord.* When Israel is poor, low,
weak, trembling, *seeing no loveliness nor worthiness in himself,* but
depending upon the mere mercy and tender bowels of the Lord, in
the free covenant of his love, &c., *then* is Israel safe. But when
he hath a being given him in the life, and is richly adorned
with the ornaments of life, and comes to have the power itself
in his hand to make use of, *then* is he in more danger of being
*somewhat of himself,* and of forgetting him that formed him (being
apt to make use of his gifts without such an *immediate* sense of the

giver as he had in his trembling and weak estate), and so of departing out of that *humble, tender, abased, contrite* state and temper of spirit, wherein he was still and preserved.

"Oh, dear friends! who know the preciousness of life, and desire the preservation of the Lord in your several conditions, let us fear the Lord and his goodness to us, remembering what a low ebb *we* were at when the Lord visited us, and how freely he visited, and how freely he daily preserveth, that we may not be *hardened or lifted up against the world, or against any sort of professors;* but may magnify the grace which hath made and keepeth up the difference between us and them, praying to the Lord *for them,* and watching for the hour of His mercy to them, exercising *all manner of sweetness and meekness and long-suffering towards them* in the meantime; also *pitying and bearing with all the tempted ones among ourselves,* as such who are sensible that we also may be tempted, and that understand the ground why we fall not by the temptation."

Oh what a manifestation of that charity which thinketh no evil, rejoiceth not in iniquity, but hopeth all things, believeth all things, and endureth all things, is found in the writings of this humble Disciple of Christ, who, like his blessed Master, sought not his own will or glory, neither the praise or honor of men, but was enabled to declare of a truth, "Lo! I come to do thy will, O God!" and to desire and seek the preservation of others from being carried away with those, who, through the subtilty of the serpent, might be led to *forsake the place of trembling,* exalting themselves above the power and government of Truth. The following query and answer evinces his sense of this danger, and of the means whereby we may be preserved from it.

"How may the little ones, if the Lord should suffer any (of such as have been very eminent in his service) to decline and fall, how may they be preserved from falling with him and them? Keeping to the measure of life in the particular, and not valuing others by an apprehension concerning them, but only knowing and honoring them as they are felt and discerned in the life; this will preserve every particular, that is thus ordered, from being tainted with any of their snares or derivations. O, Israel! O, little babes! *know no man after the flesh;* but the Lord alone in His living Spirit; for man is but a vessel wherein the life may appear or disappear at pleasure, and the Lord is not engaged to make use of man in his service further than he seeth good. Oh! know the life in *thine own* heart, *that* is to be the judge in thee concerning the appearance of life in others. If *that* judge not, be still and silent in thy heart, waiting for its judgment; when that judgeth, let all thy thoughts and reasoning be bowed down under it. Let man have no more than his due, while the Lord pleaseth to make use of him; and to such there will accrue no great shaking or danger, when the Lord layeth aside any of his instruments. But if anything but the life judge, it will still either *be setting up or throwing down man;* whereby will come loss on either hand in the issue, to all such who thus act."

Oh, let us cease from espousing or defending man's cause, man's wisdom, man's will, lest our glory be in our shame, and our triumph in the defeat of the ends of truth and justice; then an effectual end will be made of the envying, strife, and contention, whereby is begotten the discord, confusion, and divisions, by which the Church is being scattered, to the reproach of Truth. O, come out and be ye separate from the corruption and defilements of party, through which insubordination and disorder have been witnessed amongst us, to the turning of the feet of many out of the way of life and peace; then shall Zion come forth again in her ancient beauty, leaning upon her Beloved, fair as the moon, clear as the sun, and (to the transgressing nature) terrible as an army with banners; so that sinners in Zion shall be afraid, and fearfulness shall surprise the hypocrite.

O, that the judgment of Truth might again prevail amongst us, to the subjecting of the spirits of the unruly, who, at the instigation of the enemy, are led to rebel against the law of righteousness, to the disturbance of the peace and harmony of the Church. O, that we might again be brought into the littleness and nothingness of self, that the life and power of Truth might be exalted in our midst, enabling us to work righteousness, stop the mouths of lions, quench the violence of fire, and condemn every tongue that should rise in judgment against us; for this is the heritage of the servants of the Lord, whose righteousness *is* of him.

" Man," says Isaac Penington, " was made for God, to be *a vessel of his pleasure*, to receive his content, enjoyment, and happiness by reflection; so that man's *proper* work was to watch the

3

spring from whence he came; to be disposed of, ordered, and to be according to *his* pleasure. This was natural to man before his fall, till a *corrupt* spirit, by deceit entered him and corrupted him. And while anything of *that* corrupt spirit or fallen nature remains, he is *apt to aspire in the selfhood,* and to seek the enjoyment of what comes from the fountain (yea, and the fountain itself also) *in and according to the will and wisdom of the selfhood.* And here let man receive *what gifts soever* from God, be advanced to *ever so high* an habitation in the land of life, yea, have the very fountain itself given him; yet by this means he will corrupt, *lose,* the gift or spring, be separated from it, and adulterate with what he can still retain or gather in *his own* principle. And here do deep travellers *lose their way,* falling from their portion in the land of life, and from their enjoyments in the paradise of the pleasure of life, into the earthly and sensual spirit, holding things wisely and richly there in the *earthly* principle, *not knowing the remove of their habitation thither, not thinking that they are there.*

"God was to the Jews a fountain of living waters, and when they forsook him, and trusted in lying vanities, they forsook the fountain of their own mercies. They then forsook the fountain of living waters, digging *to themselves* broken cisterns that could hold no water." And so it is now with those who turn aside from the leadings and drawings of the Holy Spirit, into the exercise of their own wills and wisdom concerning themselves or others, who are led, by the spirit of the world, to depart from the doctrines, government, or order of Truth—they separate themselves from the fountain of life and forsake their own mercies.

Herein is our unity with the life destroyed. "When anything of the earthly nature comes between the soul and the life, this interrupts the soul's unity with the life itself, and it also interrupts its unity with the life in others, and the unity of the life in others with it. Anything of the man's spirit, of the man's wisdom, of the man's will, not bowed down and brought into subjection, and so not coming forth in and under the authority and guidance of life, in this is somewhat of the nature of division; yea, the very knowledge of truth, and holding it forth by the man's wisdom, and in his will, out of the movings and power of life, brings a damp upon the life, and interrupts the unity; for the life in others cannot unite with this *in spirit,* though it may own the words to be true."

Herein is the "recovery of Israel from any degree of loss in any kind, at any time. This is the way of restoring unity to Israel, upon a sense of the want thereof; even *every one retiring in his own particular, and furthering the retirings of others to the principle of life,* that every one *there* may feel the washing from what hath in any measure corrupted, and the new-begetting into the power of life. From this the true and lasting unity will spring amain, to the gladdening of all hearts that know the sweetness of it, and who cannot but naturally and most earnestly desire it. Oh! mark, therefore, the way is not by striving to beget into one and the same apprehension concerning things, nor by endeavoring to bring into the same practices; but by alluring and drawing into *that* wherein the unity consists, and which brings it forth in the vessels which are seasoned therewith and ordered thereby.

"Unity in the life is the ground of true brotherly love and fellowship; not that another man walks just as I do; though he be weaker or stronger, yet he walks by the same principles of light, and is felt in the same Spirit of life which guideth both the weak and the strong in their several ranks, order, and proper way and place of subjection to that one Spirit of life and truth which all are to be subject to.

"Nay, he that *is* truly spiritual and strong in the light and spirit of the Lord, *cannot* desire that the weak should walk just as he does, but only as they are led thereunto by the same Spirit that strengthened, taught, and led him.

"When his disciples had been all scattered from Him upon his death, he did not afterward upbraid them, but sweetly gathered them. O, dear friends! have we received the same life of sweetness? Let us bring forth *the same sweet fruits,* being ready to excuse and to receive what may tend towards the excuse of another in any doubtful case; and where there is any evil manifest, wait, O! wait to *overcome it with good.* O! let us not spend the strength of our spirits in crying out of one another because of evil; but watch and wait when the mercy and the healing virtue will please to arise. O Lord, my God, when thou hast shown the wants of Israel in any kind sufficiently (whether in the particular, or in the general), bring forth the supply thereof from thy fulness so ordering in thine eternal wisdom, that all may be ashamed and abased before thee and thy name praised *in and over all.*"

O, let us come out and be separate from the sin and iniquity of *our own* hearts, that we may become united to Christ, our holy head, in his *inward* appearance, whereby alone we can know of spiritual unity one with another. Let us come home and keep home to the witness for God within *our own* souls, and be taught of him the way of salvation from the deceit and power of sin, by which we are so often betrayed into self-love, self-exaltation, and bigotry, and from thence into contempt and scorn, to the loss of the badge of discipleship, and our evidence of the new birth being brought forth in us, which is to be felt and known in the experience of the unfeigned love of the brethren, whereby our hearts are enlarged, and enabled to embrace the whole creation in our prayers for Divine mercy and preservation, and restrained from limiting the grace and power of God within the narrow boundary of human comprehension—from limiting the Holy One of Israel, either as it respects the workings of his Holy Spirit in us or others, or the number of those he may be pleased to add to his name.

Let us remember for our admonition, the sorrow of David for having numbered the people; for it is written of him that his heart smote him after he had done this thing; wherefore he cried unto the Lord, saying, "I have greatly sinned in *that* I have done; and now I beseech thee, O Lord, take away the iniquity of thy servant, for I have done very foolishly." And when the Lord smote the people for the sin of their king, how did David intercede for them, saying, " Lo, I have sinned, and done wickedly; but these sheep, what have they done? Let thine hand, I pray thee, be against me, and against my father's house." And David made an offering unto the Lord that the plague might be stayed from the people; a costly offering; for he refused to offer unto the Lord his God of that which cost him nothing. "So the Lord was entreated for the land, and the plague was stayed from Israel."

Is there not a lesson of instruction in this for those among the leaders of the people, who have opened their hearts to the suggestions of that limiting and dividing spirit, which would be separating between the members of the visible Church, and pronouncing the judgment of apostacy upon all those who are not prepared to unite in bringing railing accusation against such as are deemed the enemies and opposers of truth? contrary to the example of humility and fear shown forth by Michael the Archangel, who, " when contending with the Devil, durst not bring against him a railing accusation," but committed all judgment unto the great Judge of us all, saying, " The *Lord* rebuke thee."

But, oh! mark the difference between him and those who kept not their first estate, of whom it is testified that they spake evil of those things which they knew not ; and the woe is pronounced upon them because they had "gone in the way of Cain, and ran greedily after the error of Baalam for a reward, and perished in the gainsaying of Core.  These, said the Apostle, are spots in your feasts of charity, when they feast with you, feeding themselves without fear ; clouds without water, carried about of winds ; trees whose fruit withereth ; raging waves of the sea, foaming out their own shame.  These are murmurers, complainers, walkers after their own lusts, and their mouth speaketh *great swelling words*, having men's persons in admiration because of advantage.  These be they who separate themselves, sensual, having not the Spirit ;" as it is written, " If ye have not the Spirit of Christ ye are none of his."

And another Apostle in speaking of the rebellious, who despise government, says of them : " Presumptuous are they, *self-willed ;* they are not afraid to speak evil of dignities ; whereas angels, which are greater in power, bring not railing accusation against them before the Lord.  But these," said he, " speak evil of the things that they understand not.  Spots they are and blemishes, sporting themselves with their own deceivings while they feast with you, beguiling unstable souls, having forsaken the right way and gone astray, following the way of Balaam, the son of Bosor, who loved the wages of unrighteousness, but was rebuked for his iniquity ; the dumb ass, speaking with man's voice, forbade the madness of the prophet.  When they speak great swelling words of vanity, they allure those that *were* clean escaped from them who live in error.  While they promise liberty, they themselves are the servants of corruption ; for of whom a man is overcome, of the same is he brought in bondage."

Does it not therefore behoove us to seek to dwell low in the valley of humility, where the blessing of the Lord is known to rest, remembering the favors bestowed upon the prophets and apostles who were brought under subjection to the Divine will and government, casting their burden upon the Lord, and not being offended or murmuring because of the crossing of their own wisdom and wills ?

Does it not concern us to be on our guard, lest we become the servants of our own hearts' lusts, and martyrs to the cruel power of corruption and deceit in the unholy cause of persecution and oppression? in the furtherance of which the enemy of our happiness and peace is seeking to divide and scatter us, in order that he may more successfully defeat the end of the Gospel, by raising and promoting in our hearts the destroying power of enmity, whereby the Holy seed and Word of life is kept under, and oppressed, while the Spirit and power of death and darkness is brought into dominion, and reigneth and ruleth in triumph in the hearts of the unbelievers, who are trusting in an arm of flesh for their deliverance from the afflictions of the suffering body of Christ, are seeking to remove the hedge which the Lord, in his wisdom and goodness, hath set about us, for our preservation, and establish bounds of *their own*, either of wider or narrower extent, as may best promote the cause they have mutually espoused, even that of party, in opposition to that of Truth.

Here two extremes meet in the support and defence of the same cause, even in the subversion of the law and order of Truth, and the exaltation of the will and wisdom of man, against which they profess to bear a mutual testimony. And in the progress of this deceitful and deceiving work, disorder and confusion have prevailed to the sorrow of the hearts of those who have no cause of their own to plead, no wisdom or righteousness of their own to boast, no will of their own to urge or gratify, but are engaged to advance, exalt, and answer those of the great Head of the Church; and not only to the affliction and sorrow of these, but to the reproach of the Truth of our profession.

And now the cry is raised in many hearts, who are engaged in weeping because of these things, "Spare thy people, O Lord, and give not thine heritage to reproach, that the heathen should rule over them; wherefore should they say among the people, Where *is* their God?" And the Lord will hearken to the prayer of these, and "will be jealous for his land, and pity his people;" and he will answer them, and say unto *his* people, "Fear not, O land; be glad and rejoice, for the Lord will do great things. I will no more make you a reproach among the heathen. Be not afraid, be glad, ye children of Zion, and rejoice in the Lord your God. I will restore to you the years that the locust hath eaten, the canker-worm, and the caterpillar, and the palmer-worm, and ye shall eat in plenty and be satisfied, and praise the name of the Lord your God, that hath dealt so wondrously with you; and ye shall know that I am in the midst of Israel, and that I am the Lord your God, and none else; and my people shall never be ashamed."

This was the assurance of the Lord to Israel of old, after "a day of darkness and of gloominess, a day of clouds and of thick darkness;" and will yet be realized by his Church and people in a day that is at hand, if we continue faithful to that which hath shown, and is showing to us, the workings of deceit, whereby we have been betrayed into the hands of our enemies, and made to suffer the reproach and shame of the apprehended forsakings of the Lord, because of iniquity. But blessed be his holy name, the mercy and help of his almighty and merciful arm are still extended for our recovery, preservation, and safety, and he will yet " redeem Zion with judgment and her converts with righteousness," sweeping away the refuge of lies, and blotting " as a cloud our sins, and as a thick cloud our transgressions;" and our sins and iniquities will he remember no more, as we are engaged to turn again unto him whom we have offended and provoked to wrath, through our revoltings and backslidings from him,—through the setting up of our own wills and judgments, and the advocacy of them, in opposition to the evident demands of truth and justice, of which he is the author and fountain, who requireth of us that we should *deal justly, love mercy, and walk humbly with him*, using great care lest we hurt the oil and the wine, through the exercise of lordship and masteries.

The truth of the following testimony of a true believer in the order and government of Truth in the Church must be very apparent to every one who has submitted his neck to the yoke of Christ, and thereby become a member of his living body. " The right church," saith he, " hath *not* many lords, but one ; and this one and only Lord, *is* the Lord Jesus Christ; and so all the subjects of this kingdom are *fellow-servants* to one Lord, to whom they do own equal obedience, and this is a strong bond of unity ; for when there are divers lords, there are divers minds, wills, and ends, and so divers laws, and these breed divisions, dissensions, and wars among men; but where there is but one Lord, there is but one law ; and where people live by one law, under one Lord, unto whom all are equally subject, this breeds peace and union.

" Now the lordship of the Church *is* the royal prerogative of

Christ, and no creature must presume to arrogate this to himself, seeing, unto the very angels, he hath *not* put in subjection this world to come, whereof we speak. And for men, Christ hath charged his own Apostles, on this sort : '*Be not ye called masters, for One is your Master, even Christ ; but he that is greatest among you shall be your servant.*' And this same doctrine the Apostle James preacheth : 'My brethren,' saith he, '*be not many masters, knowing that ye shall receive the greater condemnation.*' Wherefore, they that are puffed up in their hearts against their *fellow-servants* might better think thus with themselves : Christ is *our* Lord as well as theirs, and is as much over us as over them, and we are not over our fellow-servants, nor they under us, but we are all alike to be commanded by him. It was the evil servant that beat his fellow-servants, upon hopes of the delay of his master's coming.

" Now they break the bond of the Church's unity, that either make themselves or others lords over the Church besides Christ, and *parcel out* this one kingdom of the Son, to *many* lords, to the great dishonor of Christ and disunion of the Church. The Pope was the first that professed himself to be the greatest master of the Church ; and most evident it is, the Church hath been most miserably lorded over, even amongst us ; and while they seek to enforce lords over the Church, they break in pieces the unity of it, even whilst they bear the simple people in hand, that they, above all other men, seek to preserve it ; but the *plurality of lords is always the cause of schisms and divisions in the Church*, which can never be one but under one lord, the Lord Jesus Christ."

In reference to the unity of the Church, our author, before referred to, says : " Unity of faith is to keep us one, notwithstanding diversity of inward gifts or outward work ; for unity of faith makes all believers righteous alike, though they differ in gifts and works ; for in Christ's kingdom each one's righteousness is reckoned by faith, and not by gifts or works. Therefore, the Apostle, having reckoned up many excellent works of the fathers, doth not enjoin us to follow these, but their faith ; saying, ' Whose faith follow, considering the end of their conversation ;' seeing the unity of the Church stands in unity of faith, and there may be unity of faith in diversity of works ; for faith uses freely any outward laws, manners, forms, works, so far as they may tend to the mortifying of our bodies and the edifying of our neighbors; wherein faith will judge for itself, and will suffer nobody to judge for it, and in all changes of works faith is the same, and changes not; and the Church still remains one, through unity of faith, in the midst of variety and diversity of outward works. And therefore where men are accounted Christians for such and such outward works' sake, and this unity of faith is not taught and received, then the gates of hell do certainly prevail.

"They that live by form in the things of God, whether it be called conformity or uniformity, do break the bond of the Church's unity; for faith doth not live upon this or that form of religion, but it lives on Christ only in every duty. The true Church is a kingdom of brethren who have all one God and Father, and all are alike dear to him. And this, truly known, will restrain believers from wronging one another, when they know that others are as dear to God as themselves, and that God hath as great and tender love to them and care over them. These will be alike near to us, because of this *one* God and Father; and so among *true* Christians there can be no such divisions, factions, and sidings, as among worldly people, because one Christian is not nearer to us than another, and so we do not take part with one against another, but, *without any respect of persons*, we embrace all that are born of God with an equal love, and *seek the good* of each one, yea, of every one, as well as any one.

"They that, being of the Church, do anything in it by *their own* spirits, and not Christ's, prejudice the peace of the Church. Therefore when any prophesy or pray in the strength of the *natural* parts, and *not* in the Spirit, they break the unity of the Church. And so those, whose hope is in earthly and carnal things, who professing to be Christians, yet live only in hopes of *worldly* profit, honor, preferment, and the attaining and enjoyment of the things of *this* life, which they, according to the eagerness of their hopes, prosecute by all ways and means : these men break the unity of the Church.

"These," said he, "are the bonds of the true Church's unity and peace; one body, one spirit, one hope of our calling, *one Lord*, one faith, one baptism, and one God and Father of all, and there is no other bond of unity necessary for the Church, for if there had been, the Apostle being guided by the Spirit would not have omitted it. And, therefore, the more are they to blame, who, making a great noise and lifting up their voice on high for unity, peace, and agreement in the Church, yet do wholly neglect these bonds, cry up one instead of them all, and that is external uniformity; and whoever breaks that is the man with them that breaks the Church's peace, and so they exalt their single uniformity above the sevenfold unity of the Church; for a man may break all these bonds of the Church's unity, and yet be a very good member of their Church, if he only observes their uniformity. But if he break this he is a schismatic and a heretic, in *their* account, though he live in all the bonds of this true and spiritual unity.

"Whoever, of their own minds, presume to add to these, are guilty of adding to the words of the book of prophecy, and so involve themselves in the curses written in this book. And let us further know, that whoever do combine together to make themselves one, out of the fore-named unity, though they call themselves the church never so much, yet they are but *sects* and *schisms, divisions* and *factions*, rent from the true church of God; for such men choose and frame a way to themselves, whereby they *think they excel* other Christians, and so cause the simple and ignorant to follow them; by which means, both they and their followers depart from the true unity of the church. Wherever this spiritual unity is neglected, Christianity is torn in pieces into as many sects as the world and Devil pleases, till there be no footsteps left either of faith or love. So that whatever these men pretend, most certain it is that all confederacies in the church of outward orders, laws, and disciplines which are enforced by the secular power, seduced by the ecclesiastical, will never hold the church together; but all these are, and have proved, and will prove, rather a wall of partition in the church, than a bond of union; and if they seem to work union, yet it is no other than the mingling clay and iron together, which no pains nor art can perfectly compound; for all peace and union knit by other bonds than are here named is no spiritual union, neither will it stand.

"And, therefore, dear Christian believers, seeing we have those bonds of unity, all of God's own making, to make us one, let not diversity of forms and rites, which are but *sorry things of men's making*, separate and divide us; but seeing each of these bonds are able to make us one, how much one should all of them together make us ?"

Having shown wherein the unity of the church consists, and how it is broken, he proceeds to speak of the church government, which he says is twofold, " The government which God exercises *immediately* by himself, and that which he exercises *mediately* by the faithful. God is now as near his true church as ever, and supports and comforts it, and guides it as a skilful pilot, in such sort, that though the floods lift up their voice and billows against it, yet they cannot sink it; for *the Lord on high is mightier than the mighty waves of the sea;* and so still, even at this day, the Lord leads his flock through the midst of wolves and lions, yea, through the midst of devils, in admirable and invincible safety, and gives them light in darkness, counsel in difficulties, and success in all attempts above and beyond, both all the power and all the expectation of the world.

" The true power of the Church is Christ's power in the faithful, which is *not a power of violence,* but a power of influence, *not a coercive,* but a persuasive power. This power is humble, and *not proud* as worldly power is; is for edification and not for destruction, or to take away outward liberties, but seeks the good of others more than its own, even to the neglect of *its own,* even as in the cases of Moses and Paul, who sought the welfare of the brethren, even though it should cost them the sacrifice of their own lives and liberty. The faithful do all things in love, seeing that all laws without love are tyranny; they do all things for peace, and to preserve peace among the faithful, and *not* to break it.

" There is no more pestilent doctrine in the Church, than to make these things necessary which are not necessary, for thus the liberty of faith is extinguished, and the consciences of men ensnared. And as all the evils of the Church do commonly flow from the officers, so the reformation is to begin with them. And who shall reform the officers but the Church itself, seeing they will be sure to tolerate one another, because it is their own case, and they sometimes arrive to such a height that they will not be contented to be the servants, but will needs make themselves lords over Christ's flock, striving to procure and maintain the power over it. But if they prove incorrigible, the Church hath power to depose them, and the greatest necessity to do so, lest the infection of rebellion and insubordination be allowed to spread, to the corruption and defilement of the private members.

"Antichrist hath cast out the simplicity of Christian people, and brought sects into the Church, making a distinction whereby some may appear holier than others, and of another order from them. And this distinction hath proved a seminary of implacable discord and heart-burning in the Church; for hereupon some have preferred themselves above other Christians, and have sought to exercise coercive power and domination, and very tyranny over them, making themselves lords, and giving them laws, rules, &c., after *their own minds*, and agreeable to *their own ends*, and have looked upon them as men of a different sect and interest from themselves, whose prosperity was their ruin, and whose power was their enslaving; and all this has been to the making void Christian brotherhood and communion. Wherefore, the right church, to preserve in it the peace of Christ, must admit of no such distinction, but all Christians must equally remain in it, kings, priests, and prophets, unto God.

"And as equality among Christians is to be kept for the preserving of peace, so also among churches; for no church can be subjected to another, which no true church will either require or allow. Where two or three are met in Christ's name, Christ himself is among them, and the head of them; and so they can submit to nobody else, seeing Christ hath made no greater nor surer promise of his presence to anybody, than to them. The officers of the Church must be kept in subordination to the Church, and not suffered to get head over it; seeing the very nature of governing in the Church is *not dominion, but service*. All true Christians and congregations are to take Christ alike for their head, and not set up visible heads, or ringleaders of men; no, not of the best of men. We are not to set up a fellow-member as head, to the division of the body.

"Let the Church suffer none to teach among them that are *not* themselves taught of God, though they have never so great natural parts, and never so much human learning. For when they are the teachers that are taught of God, they will *only* teach the truth which they have heard and learned from God; and the line of every man's teaching must extend *no further*. But when they teach that are *not* so taught, they *will*, in many things, vary from the truth as it is in Jesus; yea, and under a form of sound doctrine, will give forth an unsound and *false sense*, to the deceiving of many that are weak and simple; and so, under the pretence of Christ, will utter the voice of a stranger, and endanger the misleading of the sheep."

These views of unity, peace, and government in the Church, shall we not do well to heed? in order to preserve harmony amongst us, and further the end for which we are associated together, and also the admonition of Isaac Penington, to "Let all strive to excel in tenderness, and in long-suffering, and to be kept out of all hard and evil thoughts one of another, and from harsh interpretations concerning anything relating to one another, remembering how many weaknesses the Lord doth pass by in us, and how ready he is to interpret everything well concerning his disciples, that may bear a good interpretation! ' The spirit,' saith he, ' is willing, but the flesh is weak.' " O, let us be persuaded by the mercies of God to our own souls, to judge *righteous* judgment, remembering ourselves, lest we also be tempted, bearing in mind, how, that in time past, we have been ensnared by the enemy, and brought into captivity to the prince and power of the air, being exalted in our own minds above the little pure witness for Truth, even to the usurpation of the seat of judgment, to the defilement and sorrow of our souls, and the promotion of discord, disunity, and division in the Church, to the reproach of Truth, the grief and trouble of the brethren, and the hindrance of the Gospel.

The following counsel of a friend of good order and government in the church, seeming pertinent to the design of this communication, is copied for the encouragement of those who are desiring their preservation amongst us: "Let friends meet often together, and see that Satan be withstood. Be sure that you fail not to set true judgment upon that spirit, for I know that it envies Truth's prosperity, and the saving of people's souls. Mark those that make divisions and sow discord, for the devil hath done more mischief by these things than ever he could do by whipping, branding, imprisoning, or hanging on the gallows. Labor for that which makes for peace, and also that humility may abound to that degree, that you may be enabled to wash one another's feet, and that the new commandment given by Christ may be walked in; that is, That you love one another. Labor in the power of God, and in *that*, rule over all disorderly and unruly spirits, that the government of Christ may be known to be upon his shoulders; and let those friends that are anciently convinced, be good examples in their places, that those who are young and seeking the Lord, and the knowledge of his way, may not be hurt by their examples; labor that the life of Truth may fill your hearts; for that *is it* which makes all capable to serve the Lord with acceptance. Pray take notice and call to mind respecting some that have professed the Truth in times past amongst us, but walked after the devices of their own hearts; what misery and distress came upon them, even to the end! The remembrance thereof hath often filled my heart with sorrow; yet I bless the Lord with my whole heart, because he hath given me to see that he is about to raise up such as shall serve him with a willing mind.

"Oh, let your waiting be upon the Lord in your monthly meetings, and at all other times, for wisdom and counsel to manage the Lord's business, and for a spirit of discernment, that you may distinguish between truth and error. My desire is that there be no indifferent minds, nor a putting off things one to another, nor a saying, It is not my business, or the like; for by so doing many hurtful things have crept in, which have brought in coldness of love to Truth, and to the real service of it. Labor to set up Christ's government amongst you, and then I know that whatsoever makes for Truth and the promotion of it, will be earnestly pursued. Let the Spirit bring it forth in whom it will, old or young, rich or poor, all is and will be one. Labor to be rightly exercised in mind, and that none give way to an indifferent mind, or a conceited spirit, which blinds the eye of the pure mind; but every one keep to the power [of the Holy Spirit], so in that ye will be enabled to withstand spirit and power of evil."